Max Goes to Jupiter

A Science Adventure with Max the Dog

SECOND EDITION

Jeffrey Bennett, Nick Schneider, Erica Ellingson

Illustrated by Michael Carroll

To Children Around the World:

Believe in yourself, believe in your dreams, and work hard to create a world in which we can all live together in peace as we reach for the stars.

About the New Edition
This second edition of *Max Goes to Jupiter* has been fully updated for the latest scientific discoveries about Jupiter and its moons.

Also by Jeffrey Bennett
For children:
Max Goes to the Moon
Max Goes to Mars
Max Goes to the Space Station
The Wizard Who Saved the World
I, Humanity

For grownups:
Beyond UFOs
Math for Life
What Is Relativity?
On Teaching Science
A Global Warming Primer

Textbooks:
The Cosmic Perspective
Life in the Universe
Using and Understanding Mathematics
Statistical Reasoning for Everyday Life

Editing: Joan Marsh
Design and Production: Mark Stuart Ong, Side By Side Studios

Published in the United States by
Big Kid Science
Boulder, Colorado
www.BigKidScience.com

ISBN: 978-1-937548-82-7
Also available in Spanish (ISBN 978-0-972181-96-9)

Scientific and Technical Advisors:
Dr. Bradley C. Edwards, Black Line Ascension
Dr. Richard Greenberg, University of Arizona
Dr. Marc Hairston, University of Texas, Dallas
Dr. Heidi Hammel, Space Science Institute
Dr. Rosaly Lopes, Jet Propulsion Laboratory
Dr. Robert Pappalardo, Jet Propulsion Laboratory
Joslyn Schoemer, Denver Museum of Nature & Science
Dr. John Spencer, Southwest Research Institute, Boulder
Dr. Mary Urquhart, University of Texas, Dallas

Thanks also to Jupiter moon artist Mark Gilliland, and to our friends at Columbine Hills Elementary and CREDO Academy

Special thanks to our models:
Starring *Cosmo* as Max

Nathan Schneider as Nathan

Susannah Carroll as Tori

Lado Jurkin as Commander Grant. As one of the "Lost Boys of Sudan," Mr. Jurkin spent years with other young boys forced by war to trek through African wilderness before reaching refugee camps. He hopes that his story and his appearance in this book will inspire many children to believe in their dreams.

Anousheh Ansari as Captain Anousheh. A noted entrepreneur and philanthropist, Ms. Ansari visited the International Space Station in 2006, making her the first astronaut of Iranian heritage and the first female private space explorer.

In Memoriam —
Joan Marsh (1937–2017)
Joan Marsh played an enormous role in Big Kid Science, editing all of our books and providing invaluable advice on all aspects of publishing and writing. She also touched many other lives, both in her professional career and in her extensive volunteer work. Friends called her "joyful Joan," and we all miss her.

This is the story of how Max the Dog helped humanity leap beyond the realm of the inner solar system — on a visit to explore the giant planet Jupiter and its wondrous moons.

3

The models of Earth and Jupiter on this page are shown correctly to scale.

Jupiter in the Night Sky

Have you ever seen Jupiter in the night sky? Probably so, because Jupiter outshines all the objects in the night sky except the Moon and Venus.

Of course, we don't always see Jupiter, just as we don't always see the Moon or Venus. Sometimes Jupiter lies in the same direction as the Sun, and is up (above our horizon) only in the daytime when we can't see it. At most other times, Jupiter is visible only for part of the night.

We can see Jupiter all night long only when it is directly opposite the Sun as viewed from Earth. The diagram below shows that this happens whenever Earth and Jupiter are aligned on the same side of their orbits around the Sun, which occurs about every 13 months. Notice that Jupiter is also at its closest to Earth at these times, so these are the times when Jupiter appears brightest in our night sky.

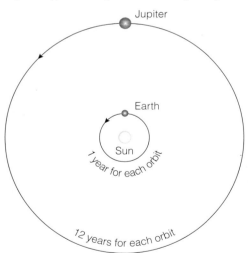

On nights when Jupiter is visible, you'll notice that it moves with the stars from east to west across the sky. We see this east-to-west movement because Earth rotates from west to east. To find out if you can see Jupiter tonight, go to www.BigKidScience.com/Jupiter.

Max was ready. His training was complete, and his spacesuit fit perfectly. In a few days, he would be bound for Jupiter. Tori, now all grown up, would be the mission's chief scientist.

Max's younger friends would stay behind, but they could see where he was going. Jupiter, king of the planets, is often the brightest object in the night sky. Tori showed the children how they could spot some of Jupiter's moons through binoculars.

Jupiter Year After Year

On any single night, Jupiter appears to stay fixed among the stars. But if you watch for many nights, you will see that Jupiter, like all the planets, appears to move gradually among the stars that make up the 12 constellations of the *zodiac*: Pisces, Aries, Taurus, Gemini, Cancer, Leo, Virgo, Libra, Scorpio, Sagittarius, Capricorn, and Aquarius. This movement is easy to understand: As Jupiter orbits the Sun, we see it in different places at different times against the distant background of stars.

Jupiter takes about 12 years to orbit the Sun, which means it also takes about 12 years to move once through all the constellations of the zodiac. It therefore moves about one constellation each year. For example, if we see Jupiter in Capricorn right now, we'll see it in Aquarius at this time next year and in Pisces the year after that.

Find out where Jupiter is located among the zodiac constellations this year by going to www.BigKidScience.com/Jupiter. What do you think you will be doing the next time Jupiter returns to the same constellation?

King of the Planets

The planet Jupiter is named for the mythological king of the gods, known as Zeus in ancient Greece and as Jupiter in ancient Rome. In Northern Europe, Jupiter was known as Thor, so *Thursday* (Thor's day) really means "Jupiter's day."

Today, we call Jupiter the "king of the planets," because it is more massive than *all* the rest of the planets combined. The photos below compare Jupiter and Earth in size. Notice that Earth could fit easily inside Jupiter's Great Red Spot, which is a giant storm with hurricane-like winds.

Great Red Spot

Just as the Sun is orbited by many planets, Jupiter is orbited by many moons (69 known moons as of 2017). Jupiter also has a thin set of rings made of countless tiny pieces of rock and dust. However, unlike Saturn's spectacular rings, Jupiter's rings are dark, thin, and very difficult to see — which is why we do not show them in this book.

Max was a natural choice to go along on the first human trip to Jupiter. After all, it was his grandfather — also named Max — who had been the first dog to go to the Moon and Mars.

Even as a puppy, Max had loved to sit in the lap of one of his human friends, listening to stories of his grandpa's space adventures.

Now, Max sat attentively while his friend Nathan talked about Jupiter's importance in human history.

"Jupiter has always been important in myth," he said, "but about 400 years ago it helped change the entire course of human history. I know it sounds a little silly now, but at that time almost everyone believed that Earth was the center of the universe."

The "Geocentric" Universe

Nathan is right: As recently as about 400 years ago, most people assumed that the Sun, planets, and stars all revolved around Earth. Because *geo* means "Earth," this ancient idea of an Earth-centered universe is usually called the "geocentric" universe.

The idea of a geocentric universe may sound silly to us today, but it seemed to make sense at the time. The daily rise and set of the Sun, Moon, planets, and stars make it *look* like all these objects are circling around us each day, and we cannot feel the constant motion of our planet as it rotates on its axis and orbits around the Sun.

So how did we learn that Earth is actually a planet orbiting the Sun? The answer is through *science*. Science is a way of observing the world carefully and using these observations to learn how things work. By about 400 years ago, new techniques had greatly improved the accuracy of planetary observations compared to those made in ancient times. Scientists soon realized that these new observations could not be explained with a geocentric universe, but made perfect sense if Earth was a planet going around the Sun. As we'll see on the next page, observations of Jupiter played a key role in this realization.

Ganymede

"Well," continued Nathan, "in 1609 a man named Galileo built a telescope and started using it to study space. Galileo made many amazing discoveries, but I think the most important was when he found four moons orbiting around Jupiter. You know what that meant, right?"

Max, who was playing with a treat, appeared to have no idea.

Galileo

Galileo Galilei, almost always known by his first name, lived from 1564 to 1642. He made so many important discoveries that he is considered one of the greatest scientists of all time. He was the first scientist to use a telescope for observing the sky, and his observations helped prove that Earth is a planet going around the Sun, rather than being the center of the universe.

Galileo's observations of Jupiter were especially important. Through his telescope, he saw four points of light near Jupiter. Watching night after night, he soon realized that these points of light were moons orbiting around Jupiter — and not around Earth. This was the first absolute proof that Earth is *not* the center of everything. Today, you need only a set of binoculars to reproduce this famous discovery. The activity on Page 30 describes how you can do it.

"It was proof that not everything in the universe goes around the Earth, and it helped convince people that our Earth is just one planet orbiting one star, and *not* the center of everything."

Max, exhibiting his troublesome streak (something his grandpa never had), jumped again and almost knocked Nathan over.

We Are NOT the Center of the Universe

Over the past 400 years we've learned not only that Earth is just one planet orbiting the Sun, but also that our solar system is just one among billions of solar systems in the Milky Way Galaxy and that our galaxy is just one among billions of galaxies in the universe. This obviously represents a dramatic change in human knowledge of our place in the universe. But should it affect the way we behave?

Different people have different answers to this question, but it may help to think about your own life. When you were very little, you probably thought that everything in the universe should revolve around *you*. But once you realized that everyone has similar thoughts and feelings, you probably learned to treat other people with more kindness and respect.

The authors of this book believe that wars, crimes, hatred, and other bad things are often caused by people who act as though they still think the universe should revolve around them. Perhaps someday, everyone will learn to accept that we really are *not* the center of the universe, and as a result we'll be able to create a better world for all of us — a world like the one we imagine in this book, in which people of all nations can work together on an amazing voyage to the planet Jupiter.

Moon Shapes

Have you ever wondered why the world is round? Jupiter's moons offer clues.

Most of Jupiter's many moons are only a few kilometers across. These small moons look rather like giant potatoes, with a variety of shapes. Jupiter's only round moons are the four moons discovered by Galileo, known together as the "Galilean moons." These four moons are much larger than the others (which is why Galileo could see them through his small telescope). In fact, they are large enough that we'd probably call them planets if they orbited the Sun. But anything that orbits a planet is always called a "moon."

Perhaps you've now guessed the key clue: Large worlds are round, but small worlds are not. You can understand why by thinking about gravity, which is what holds a world together. Small worlds, such as Jupiter's small moons and most asteroids, have barely enough gravity to keep them from falling apart. Larger worlds, such as the Galilean moons, have much stronger gravity. Because gravity always pulls toward a world's center, it forces any large world into a round shape. That is not only why the Galilean moons are round, but also why Earth and all the other planets are round.

Io   Europa   Ganymede   Callisto

Max wasn't done yet, but neither was Nathan. "Today," he concluded, "we know that Jupiter actually has dozens of moons. But the four discovered by Galileo — called Io, Europa, Ganymede, and Callisto — are by far the biggest of them all."

The class applauded, just as Max collided with Nathan and they crashed together to the ground.

Hoping that would be the last crash, Max and his friends were soon off to a new, human-made island in the eastern Pacific Ocean. There, they boarded the Space Elevator, which would carry them straight up for almost three days, until they were some 100,000 kilometers (60,000 miles) above Earth.

The elevator rose faster than a jet airplane, but they felt little sensation of motion. They just watched Earth drop away as they rose, and noticed their weight gradually lessen with the weakening gravity.

A Space Elevator?

"Hold on," you may be thinking, "can the authors really be serious about an elevator going 100,000 kilometers straight up into space?"

Yes, we can, and it's easy to understand why. Today, it's very expensive to launch anything into space. A rocket must go fast enough to escape Earth's gravity, which requires a lot of fuel. But the fuel itself weighs a lot, which means you need even more fuel to get the whole rocket going. The result is that it takes a huge, expensive rocket to launch even a small spaceship. With an elevator, we wouldn't need a big rocket at all. We'd use electricity to move the elevator, and we could generate that electricity with solar panels in space.

Here's how it would work: It turns out that satellites at an altitude of about 36,000 kilometers (22,000 miles) above Earth's equator orbit at precisely the same speed that Earth rotates, which means they always stay directly above the same spot on Earth. With strong enough cables, we could build an elevator direct from the equator to this *geosynchronous orbit*. By extending the elevator even higher, as in this story, we could essentially "fling" a spaceship from the top of the elevator toward a distant planet.

Many scientists and engineers believe we will soon have the technology needed to build a space elevator, and some think it could be built for less than the cost of one year's NASA budget. Let's hope they are right, and look forward to elevator rides to space.

The Elevator Ride

What would it be like to ride an elevator to space?

At first, it would feel like a ride in a normal elevator, except that being outdoors the elevator would be buffeted by winds. Rising at the speed of a fast car, it would take about an hour to get above most of Earth's atmosphere. At that point, you'd be in space, where there'd be no more wind and you could see stars even in the daytime.

The elevator could then go much faster, since there'd be no more air resistance. For the three-day trip in this story, the elevator goes up at about 1,300 kilometers per hour (800 mi/hr), which is faster than a jet plane. The elevator would have to be large enough to have rooms for sleeping and eating.

You'd feel your weight gradually lessen as you rose, but you'd be completely weightless only when you reached geosynchronous altitude (36,000 km). There, the elevator's speed (moving with Earth's rotation) would match the speed of an orbiting satellite or spaceship, so you'd float freely in the elevator cabin. Beyond that, something called "centrifugal force" would actually make you feel a bit of weight again, but "up" and "down" would be reversed: The floor would become the ceiling, and the ceiling would be the floor.

Throughout the journey, you would see Earth gradually falling away into the distance. By the time you reached the top, Earth would look about the way it does in the painting on this page. It would be a beautiful view.

The Jupiter ship was anchored at the top of the elevator. Commander Grant and the rest of the crew were already on board, completing the final preparations. They were ready to go when Max and Tori arrived. It was time for the children to say good-bye and take the elevator back down to Earth. Children might someday go to Jupiter, but the first trip could take only grown-up astronauts — and one dog.

Tori was in charge of the daily video broadcasts back to Earth, telling children about the trip. "Jupiter is really far away," she explained. "It is more than five times as far from the Sun as Earth, which means our trip from Earth to Jupiter is almost *two thousand times* as far as a trip from Earth to the Moon. That's why it will take us months to get there, even though our ship has the most powerful rocket engines ever built."

"Our ship gives us artificial gravity by rotating," she continued, "but it doesn't feel quite the same as being on Earth. Commander Grant says it makes him feel like a hamster on a wheel. But you can see that it doesn't bother Max!"

A Trip to Jupiter

Tori is right about Jupiter's great distance, which we can visualize with a scale model of the solar system. The *Voyage* model in Washington, DC (www.voyagesolarsystem.org) shrinks our solar system down *10 billion times*, so that the Sun is the size of a large grapefruit and pinhead-size Earth orbits it about 15 meters (16.5 yards) away. Our Moon (even smaller than Earth) is only about 4 centimeters (1.5 inches) from Earth — which means Earth and the orbit of the Moon could fit in the palm of your hand. To reach marble-size Jupiter, however, you have to walk about 75 meters (80 yards) from the model Sun.

In fact, Jupiter is so far away that we'll need new rocket technologies to make the round trip in a reasonable amount of time. The paintings in this story show a ship powered by nuclear energy.

The ship's main cabin is shaped like a donut so that it can rotate to provide artificial gravity. It isn't really gravity, but it feels much the same. You can understand the idea by imagining holding tight on a fast merry-go-round: You get flung to the outside, which therefore feels like "down." The ship only has to rotate about once or twice a minute to provide the same effect, which is why Max and the astronauts live with "down" toward the *outside* of the donut and "up" toward its center.

13

As the ship approached Jupiter, the crew fired the rocket engines, slowing their speed until Jupiter's gravity could hold them in orbit. They stared out the windows in awe as they orbited around Jupiter for the first time.

The View from Jupiter

The painting on this page shows what it really would look like as the spaceship swung into orbit around Jupiter, so that Jupiter appeared as a thin crescent. As Captain Anousheh points out, we can even see Earth shining faintly in the distance; it is the tiny blue dot below Jupiter on the right-hand page.

The story's reference to a "mote of dust" comes from a famous quote by astronomer Carl Sagan. At Dr. Sagan's suggestion, NASA used the *Voyager 1* spacecraft to take a photo (below) of Earth from the outskirts of our solar system. Earth is the tiny dot; the surrounding "sunbeam" was created by light scattering in *Voyager*'s camera. About the dot in this photo, Sagan wrote: "That's here. That's home. That's us. On it, everyone you ever heard of, every human being who ever lived, lived out their lives . . . on a mote of dust, suspended in a sunbeam." (See the complete quote at www.BigKidScience.com/Jupiter.)

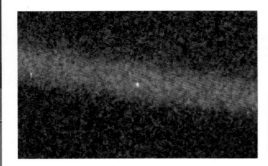

Captain Anousheh was the first to notice Earth in the distance. She couldn't help but marvel at the sight, especially as she thought about the different nationalities of all the crew members.

"It sure makes you think," she said. "We all come from countries that used to fight each other. Now, we are all working together here, in a tiny ship from which our whole planet looks barely as large as a mote of dust."

Their first science mission called for dropping a probe into Jupiter's atmosphere. Tori explained the goals. "We can't land on Jupiter because it doesn't have a solid surface, and its winds are too strong to allow us to take a ship into its atmosphere. So we're going to send in this robotic probe, which will radio back information about Jupiter's clouds, winds, and gases."

The rest of the crew prepared the probe. No one noticed Max's ball slipping into the airlock, just before they closed the door.

No Solid Surface

Do you know why the cover of this book shows Max on one of Jupiter's moons (Europa), rather than on Jupiter itself? As Tori explains, the answer is that Max couldn't land on Jupiter even if he wanted to, because there's no solid ground.

Earth has a solid surface because it is made mostly of metal and rock. The same is true of the Moon and the planets Mercury, Venus, and Mars. Jupiter is very different: It is made mostly of hydrogen and helium, along with a few other substances that give its clouds their beautiful colors. If you descended into Jupiter's atmosphere, you would continue down and down and never hit ground. Unfortunately, you wouldn't survive long, because the pressure and temperature rise rapidly with depth. After descending beneath the clouds, you'd soon be crushed by the growing pressure.

In principle, a ship could use a balloon to float in Jupiter's atmosphere, just as the probe does in this story. But while a balloon flight on Jupiter is fine for a robotic probe, it wouldn't be very comfortable for people or dogs: Jupiter's winds are so strong that they would make a hurricane on Earth seem like a gentle breeze by comparison. And because there's no solid ground, you'd have no hope of ever finding any shelter.

AIRLOCK CLOSE ↓

The crew watched excitedly as the probe shot out toward Jupiter. Equipped with a balloon, the probe would float in Jupiter's atmosphere for months.

Max, looking out a different window at his escaping soccer ball, had other concerns. (Fortunately, Tori had brought a few extra balls along.)

Missions to Jupiter

Like all the planets, Jupiter has never yet been visited by humans or animals. However, several robotic spacecraft have visited Jupiter, using radio to send pictures and other data back to scientists on Earth.

The first spacecraft to photograph Jupiter up close was *Pioneer 10*, which flew past Jupiter in 1973. *Pioneer 11* followed a year later, and two more spacecraft — *Voyager 1* and *Voyager 2* — flew past Jupiter in 1979. All four of these spacecraft continued outward after passing Jupiter and are now on their way out of our solar system.

Three other spacecraft have also flown past Jupiter, using its powerful gravity to help "slingshot" them on to their primary destinations: *Ulysses* (on its way to fly over the poles of the Sun), *Cassini* (on its way to Saturn), and *New Horizons* (on its way to Pluto and beyond).

Our most detailed study of Jupiter has come from two orbiting missions. The *Galileo* spacecraft orbited Jupiter from 1995 to 2003, taking thousands of photographs of Jupiter and its moons and sending a small probe into Jupiter's atmosphere. More recently, the *Juno* spacecraft has been studying Jupiter from a polar orbit since 2016. Several other missions are in various stages of development (as of 2018), including the European Space Agency's *Jupiter Icy Moons Explorer* and NASA's *Europa Clipper*. Be on the lookout for news from these exciting missions.

The Volcano World

Io, the nearest to Jupiter of the four Galilean moons, is sometimes called the "volcano world" because it has more active volcanoes than any other planet or moon in the solar system. Io usually has several volcanoes erupting at the same time, which is why Max could have accidentally gotten so close to a lava river.

Although the molten lava is red hot, the rest of Io's surface is quite cold because Jupiter and its moons are so far from the Sun. So while the volcanoes spew out lots of gas, most of this gas quickly cools and condenses, falling to the surface as bits of dust or icy "snow." The dust is made mostly of sulfur, which gives Io its orange and red colors, and sulfur dioxide snow coats the surface with a whitish frost.

As shown in the upper left of the painting, Jupiter dominates Io's sky. Although Io is about the same distance from Jupiter as our Moon from Earth, Jupiter is so big that on Io it would appear to be about 40 times as large across as the full moon on Earth, or about as big as a dinner plate held at arm's length.

Aside from Jupiter, Io's sky is black even in the daytime, because Io has too little atmosphere to scatter much sunlight. Remember also that because Jupiter and Io are five times as far from the Sun as Earth, daylight on Io is not very bright. That's why Max has a flashlight on the front of his spacesuit.

Although Max and the crew could not land on Jupiter, they could visit its moons. Their first stop was Io. They left the main ship in orbit while they descended to the surface in a small lander.

As they walked on the bizarre surface, Tori reported back to children on Earth. "When I say *moon*," she said, "you probably think of a barren and cratered world like our own Moon. But Io is not like that at all. As you can see, Io has volcanoes all over the place. And the ground is covered by this sticky dust. I've got to keep wiping my helmet visor so I can see."

Unable to wipe the dust from his helmet, Max could not see where he was going. He heard Tori's call in his helmet radio, but he did not know which direction she was calling from. He was lost, and wandering dangerously close to a river of hot lava.

Why Does Io Have So Many Volcanoes?

Believe it or not, you can understand why Io has so many volcanoes by starting with this very different question: Have you ever noticed how hot potatoes take longer to cool off than hot peas? The same idea holds for planets and moons. That is why our relatively large Earth is still hot enough inside to have active volcanoes, while our much smaller Moon has not had significant volcanic activity for at least about three billion years. But Io is barely bigger than our Moon. How, then, can it still be so hot inside that it is covered by active volcanoes?

The answer is related to the reason we have tides on Earth. Our tides are caused by the Moon's gravity, which pushes and pulls not only on the oceans but on Earth's insides as well.

Io has tides that push and pull on its insides in much the same way, except these tides are much stronger than Earth's tides because they are created by Jupiter's much stronger gravity. These tides vary in strength as Io goes around its elliptical (oval-shaped) orbit of Jupiter, so Io's insides are flexed back and forth about four times a week. This flexing generates so much friction and heat that it has kept Io very hot on the inside for billions of years — hot enough to melt interior rock that then erupts upward to make Io's many volcanoes.

Dancing Moons

You probably know that gravity is what holds planets and moons in their orbits, and on Page 19 we talked about how gravity causes tides. In fact, gravity can have many other important effects.

For example, gravity explains why our Moon always keeps nearly the same face toward Earth: Long ago, the Moon probably rotated much more rapidly, but Earth's gravity created tidal bulges on the Moon. These bulges generated friction that slowed the Moon's rotation until the bulges stayed aligned with Earth, and this alignment is what keeps the same side of the Moon facing Earth at all times. Jupiter's gravity has affected its moons similarly, so that Io, Europa, Ganymede, and Callisto all keep the same side toward Jupiter at all times.

Even more amazingly, the orbits of these moons were altered over time by their gravitational pulls on each other, so the three inner moons now "dance" together: Io completes exactly four orbits in the time it takes Europa to complete two orbits and Ganymede to complete one. In fact, this dance causes the orbits to be elliptical, and therefore is responsible for the tidal flexing that heats these moons on the inside.

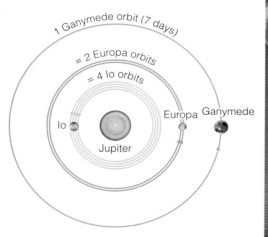

Luckily, Commander Grant saved the day, reaching Max just in time. Everyone was glad to get back to the lander.

Tori had a little talk with Max as the lander rose up from Io to return to the main ship. She hoped he would behave better at their next stop, which would be the science highlight of their trip.

As they approached Europa, Tori broadcast her report back to Earth. "Wow," she began. "You can probably see in the pictures that this is no ordinary moon. On the outside, Europa is made mostly of ice, meaning frozen water."

"But that's only the beginning of the excitement," she continued. "Although we can't see it, we're almost sure that there's a giant ocean of liquid water under all that ice. In fact, we think there's more ocean water on Europa than on Earth!"

"I can hardly wait to go down to the surface," said Tori. "We're going to try to find a spot where the ice is thinner, and launch our robotic submarine from there."

The Water World

As Tori explains, scientists really do think that Europa has a deep ocean of liquid water underneath its icy surface. But since we can't see through the ice, how can we think there's an ocean?

We know that Europa's surface is made mostly of water (H_2O) ice. We also know that Europa experiences the same type of "tidal heating" as Io. This heating is less extreme on Europa because it is farther from Jupiter, but it should still create enough warmth to keep water melted beneath an outer "crust" of ice.

Close-up photos of Europa's surface support this idea, showing regions where it appears that the icy crust has broken up and refrozen (see photo below). In other places it appears that ocean water has leaked through cracks in the crust and then frozen.

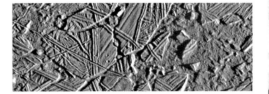

More evidence comes from careful studies of magnetic fields around Europa, which tell us that Europa has a liquid layer beneath its icy crust.

Putting all these clues together, scientists conclude that Europa *probably* has a subsurface ocean more than 50 kilometers (30 miles) deep, hidden beneath up to 25 kilometers (15 miles) of solid ice. If so, then Europa may have two to three times as much ocean water as Earth!

How will we learn *for sure* if the ocean exists? Only by sending more spacecraft to study Europa in greater detail.

Icy Moons

You may be surprised to learn that Europa has so much ice and water, but H_2O is actually common in the solar system. The reason is easy to understand.

Scientists learn what distant objects are made of by carefully studying their light (using a technique called *spectroscopy*). In this way, scientists have learned that the chemical elements hydrogen and helium are by far the two most common ingredients of stars and their planetary systems. That is why the Sun and large planets like Jupiter are made mostly of hydrogen and helium. (Smaller objects, like Earth, do not have strong enough gravity to hold on to hydrogen and helium gas.)

The next three most common elements are carbon, nitrogen, and oxygen. All three of these can combine with hydrogen to make molecules that are therefore also common in planetary systems: Hydrogen combines with carbon to make methane (CH_4), with nitrogen to make ammonia (NH_3), and with oxygen to make water (H_2O).

When our solar system was forming about 4½ billion years ago, temperatures around Jupiter were cold enough for water to freeze into solid ice, which is why Europa and most of the rest of Jupiter's moons (except Io) contain lots of water ice. Farther out, where it was even colder, moons of Saturn, Uranus, and Neptune ended up with other kinds of ice as well.

The lander carried Max and the crew down to Europa's hard, icy surface. There was no dust here, but plenty of dangerous cliffs and crevasses. Still, Tori figured Max could see, so she let him bring a ball to play with in the weak gravity.

The crew was busy, using sensors to measure the thickness of the ice in different places. Several minutes went by before anyone noticed that Max was missing. "Oh no, not again," sighed Tori.

They found him more than a kilometer away, where he'd chased after his ball as it had rolled downhill. Tori began to scold him: "Max, are we going to have to leave you on the ship?"

But Commander Grant interrupted. "Not so fast," he said, standing over the spot where Max's ball had come to rest. "My sensor says this is the thinnest patch of ice anywhere around. Max, I think you've found the spot for our submarine!"

They brought over the submarine, turned on its heater, and watched it begin to melt its way down to the ocean below.

Exploring Europa's Ocean

Are you wondering why it takes the submarine so long to melt its way down to the ocean? Remember that, assuming it really exists, Europa's ocean is buried beneath up to 25 kilometers of solid ice. Using just a small on-board heater, it will take a robotic submarine quite a while to melt its way through this ice. Moreover, the ice above the submarine will refreeze as it melts its way down, which explains why it's unlikely that any people or animals would ride along. After all, it wouldn't be much fun to be stuck within all that ice for a few weeks.

Once the submarine reached the ocean, it could travel just like a submarine in Earth's oceans. But it would be dark everywhere, because no sunlight gets through the thick ice above. That is why the painting shows only the lights from the sub itself.

Unless there is life, there won't be much to see in the deep ocean water. But the ocean bottom could be very interesting. There, the same tidal heating that keeps the ocean water from freezing might power underwater volcanoes, which could erupt much like volcanic vents found on Earth's ocean floor. In this painting, we've imagined that these undersea volcanoes really exist on Europa, and we see one as it erupts.

Back aboard the ship, Tori spoke to children on Earth about what the submarine would do. "It will take a few weeks for the submarine to melt its way down into the ocean," she said, "and then it will start transmitting pictures and other information back to us and to Earth. We can tell it where to go. We'll start by having it dive deep in search of undersea volcanoes. And of course, we'll be on the lookout for any signs of life. Do you think we'll find any?"

With their most important task accomplished, the crew decided to head for home. They flew past Ganymede so they could get a good look at the largest moon in the solar system, but they did not land there. Ganymede, Callisto, and Jupiter's many smaller moons would get their first footprints from future explorers.

There was little to see out their windows on the long trip home, so they often watched the screen showing the video feed from the submarine. It was mostly dull, but one day . . .

Ganymede and Callisto

Max and the crew don't stop at Ganymede or Callisto in this story, but scientists are still very interested in these moons.

Ganymede is the largest of the four Galilean moons. In fact, it is the largest moon in our solar system, and it is larger than the planet Mercury. Like Europa, Ganymede has a surface made mostly of water ice, and it is possible that Ganymede also has an ocean beneath a thick, icy crust.

Callisto is a little smaller than Ganymede (but larger than either Io or Europa) and also has a surface of water ice. Like our Moon's surface, Callisto's surface is covered with impact craters, which are scars left by the crashes of asteroids or comets. Because these crashes were most common when the solar system was young, Callisto's many craters tell scientists that its surface must still look much as it did almost 4 billion years ago. For that reason, it seems unlikely that any liquid water ever wells up from below on Callisto. Nevertheless, it is still possible that Callisto also has a hidden ocean far beneath its surface, and scientists hope to learn more about this possibility with future missions to Jupiter.

Is There Really Life on Europa?

In this story, the submarine beams back video of living creatures swimming in Europa's subsurface ocean. But is there really life on Europa?

No one knows, but if the ocean is real, then life is a real possibility, especially if the ocean bottom has volcanic vents like the one shown on Page 24. On Earth, these deep ocean vents are home to amazing communities of life, and many biologists suspect that life on Earth originated around such vents. If so, perhaps life could have originated in the same way around volcanic vents in Europa's ocean.

Most scientists suspect that if Europa has life at all, it will be microscopic or very simple life. Still, because we can't see through the ice, we can't completely rule out the possibility of finding much larger or more complex creatures.

In fact, one author of this book used to say that "for all we know, there could be *whales* swimming in Europa's ocean." He no longer says this, however, and can you guess why? It's because a 10-year-old once reminded him that whales need air to breathe, and therefore could not live in an ocean covered everywhere by thick ice! So thanks to this child's reminder, the author now says "there could be *really big fish* swimming in Europa's ocean."

Of course, the best way to find out whether fish or any other life exists in Europa's ocean is to go there, perhaps sending a submarine down through the ice just as Max and the crew do in this story.

They were all sleeping when Max started to bark. He ran over and licked Tori's face until she got up. Then he woke Commander Grant, and then the rest of the crew. Long afterward, people still argued about whether it was a coincidence or whether Max really paid attention to the video screen. But coincidence or not, there was no doubt about what the crew saw on the screen: Living creatures were swimming in the ocean of Europa.

Max was a hero, just like his grandpa before him. Best of all, the work wasn't finished, because the robotic explorers continued to send pictures and information back from Jupiter. There was so much to analyze that children around the world were soon making their own discoveries — and dreaming about their own trips to new worlds.

Space Data for Education

The painting on this page shows children in a rural village working on laptops to examine real data about Jupiter. But is that really possible?

The answer is *yes*! Today, anyone with an Internet connection has access to almost all the data ever collected by space missions. With a bit of Web searching, you can find all the images and data from the *Galileo* and *Juno* missions to Jupiter, and much, much more. You can explore these data for yourself, and perhaps even make a new discovery.

Many people are already working to spread this type of education worldwide. For example, the "one laptop per child" project hopes to eventually ensure laptop access to all children, in even the poorest countries.

So if you ever get sad about the many problems that we face in this world, such as war, hatred, poverty, or global warming, try instead to focus on the great possibilities that await us if we can work together to solve these problems. Perhaps before long, children everywhere really will be able to work together to learn about the universe, and then grow up to take incredible journeys to places like Jupiter and beyond.

As for Max, he was just glad to get back home. It was his friends who understood the significance of it all. There may be life on other worlds, but no other known world has anything like the teeming life that thrives in every imaginable place on our home planet.

Thanks to Max, they understood better than ever that Earth is a living planet, and that all of our lives depend on taking good care of this remarkable world.

29

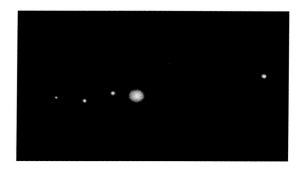

Figure 1: View of Jupiter and the Galilean moons through a small telescope.

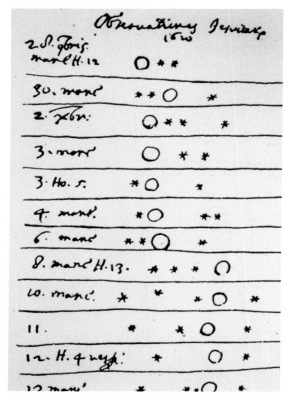

Figure 2: A page from Galileo's notebook written in 1610. His sketches show four "stars" near Jupiter (the circle) but in different positions at different times (and sometimes hidden from view). Galileo soon realized that the "stars" were actually orbiting Jupiter.

Seeing Jupiter's Moons for Yourself

Would you like to see for yourself what Galileo saw through his telescope? All you need is a good pair of binoculars (or a telescope) and a way to hold them steady (a tripod is helpful, but leaning against a railing or a car can also work).

If you are choosing binoculars, your choices will be described by two numbers, such as 7×35 or 10×50. The first number is the magnification; for example, "$7 \times$" means that objects will look 7 times larger through the binoculars than to your eye. The second number is the diameter of each lens in millimeters. A bigger lens lets in more light, so 7×50 binoculars make it easier to see Jupiter's moons than 7×35 binoculars, even though both have the same magnification.

Before you begin, make sure that Jupiter is visible by going to www.BigKidScience.com/Jupiter. If it's a good time for viewing and the sky is clear, take your binoculars (or telescope) out and point them up at Jupiter. You should be able to see two to four of the Galilean moons, looking somewhat as they do in Figure 1, though they could be anywhere in their orbits.

The key to repeating Galileo's discovery is to look through your binoculars for several nights in a row. Each night, draw a simple sketch showing Jupiter and the positions of its moons; Figure 2 shows Galileo's own drawings. By comparing your sketches over several nights, you can confirm that these moons really are orbiting Jupiter. You will then have found your own proof that Earth is *not* the center of the universe.

Learning More About Jupiter

You can learn much more about Jupiter and its moons from the Web. Be sure to look for images of Jupiter taken by some of the missions that have visited it. For a taste of what you can find, the image below shows Jupiter as seen by the *Cassini* spacecraft. Notice the spectacular patterns and colors of its clouds, as well as the Great Red Spot near the lower right. The black dot is Europa's shadow on Jupiter.

A Note to Parents and Teachers

While we hope that everything in *Max Goes to Jupiter* is self-explanatory, we thought it might help to share a little bit of our motivation for writing this book and our hopes for how it will be used.

Like all Big Kid Science books, *Max Goes to Jupiter* is designed to incorporate what we call the three pillars of successful learning: *education*, *perspective*, and *inspiration*.

- The **education** pillar is the specific content that we want students to learn. For example, in this book, the education pillar includes both the science of Jupiter (and its moons) and the historical context of its role in proving that Earth is *not* the center of the universe.
- The **perspective** pillar connects the educational content to the way readers think about their own lives and their place in the universe.
- The **inspiration** pillar builds on the educational content and perspective to help students imagine the amazing things they might do or see in the future.

We've tried to build all three pillars into every page of this book, but some pages focus more on one than the others. For example, Pages 14–15 are particularly focused on the perspective we can gain by thinking about our own planet as seen from the orbit of Jupiter, while the space elevator is an idea that should inspire students to think big about possibilities for the future. When reading this book with children, especially in classroom settings, we encourage you to use discussion or activities to help them think about the ideas behind the three pillars as you go along. The Big Kid boxes on the sides of the pages, and the activities on Pages 30 and 31, should be particularly helpful to you.

As to our own motivations for writing this book, they are simple: We want kids to understand why science is important to everyone, and we want to motivate kids to work hard so that they can achieve their own dreams. You'll have to judge for yourself whether we've accomplished these goals, but we are very honored that our book was selected for the Story Time From Space program, in which astronauts read books aloud from the International Space Station. You can watch the video of this book being read by astronaut Mike Hopkins in the video library at StoryTimeFromSpace.com.

Finally, we note that as time goes on, we hope to add more information and activities to the book website: www.bigkidscience.com/jupiter. Please check it out, and share it with others.

We hope you enjoy the book, and that you'll continue to follow the exploration of space as we all work together to reach for the stars.

— Jeffrey Bennett, Nick Schneider, and Erica Ellingson

NASA astronaut Mike Hopkins reading *Max Goes to Jupiter* in the cupola of the International Space Station. Watch the video of the reading at www.storytimefromspace.com.